It's Time to Rhyme . . .

The answer to every WORDY GURDY brain-teaser is a rhyming pair of words (like FAT CAT and DOUBLE TROUBLE) that will fit in the letter squares. The number after the definition tells you how many syllables are in each word.

. . . with **WORDY GURDY** !

#1

WORDY GURDY®

by Ricky Kane

BERKLEY BOOKS, NEW YORK

WORDY GURDY® #1

A Berkley Book / published by arrangement with
United Feature Syndicate, Inc.

PRINTING HISTORY
Berkley edition / June 1989

ISBN: 0-425-11394-9

Berkley Books are published by The Berkley Publishing Group,
200 Madison Avenue, New York, New York 10016.
The name "Berkley" and the "B" logo
are trademarks belonging to Berkley Publishing Corporation.

PRINTED IN THE UNITED STATES OF AMERICA

10 9 8 7 6 5 4 3 2 1

1. Abner (1)

2. Boy's cutting tool (1)

3. Feet fall asleep (1)

4. In a while, Benedict (2)

5. Amsterdam's boats (2)

6. Joan feels a chill (2)

7. Skinny Algonquian (2)

ANSWERS:
1. LUM CHUM 2. LADS ADZ 3. TOES DOZE 4. LATER TRAITOR
5. MOREYS DORIES 6. RIVERS SHIVERS 7. SCRAWNY SHAWNEE

1. 2, 3 in Munich (1)

2. Legal system's grasp (1)

3. Very slow letter delivery (1)

4. Wiser bet (2)

5. Bank balance (2)

6. Wrong numbers (2)

7. Wicked water boy of the sky (4)

ANSWERS:
1. ZWEI DREI 2. LAWS JAWS 3. SNAIL MAIL 4. SAGER WAGER
5. ACCOUNT AMOUNT 6. PHONERS BONERS 7. NEFARIOUS AQUARIUS

1. Seoul army medic (1)

2. Alaskan isle prohibition (2)

3. Captured stream (1)

4. Criminals' jars (1)

5. Intimidated throng (1)

6. Lazier sidestepper (2)

7. While healing (2)

ANSWERS:
1. ROK DOC 2. ATTU TABOO 3. TOOK BROOK 4. THUGS JUGS
5. COWED CROWD 6. IDLER SIDLER 7. DURING CURING

1. Concealed the unconscious (1)

2. Tan paper (1)

3. Italian money, Anne (2)

4. Has no tender envelope initials (1)

5. Crowd suffering tedium (1)

6. Certain constellation, Pat (3)

7. Belgian-French blow-ups (2)

ANSWERS:
1. HID ID 2. BEIGE PAGE 3. LIRA MEARA 4. LACKS SWAKS
5. BORED HORDE 6. ORION OBRIEN 7. WALLOONS BALLOONS

1. Stretch yarn (1)

2. Harbor defense (1)

3. Lethargic motherless calf (2)

4. Sanctuary for an expert (2)

5. Prepares to wed Coleman (2)

6. Straying sire (2)

7. Emphasizes frocks (2)

ANSWERS:
1. PULL WOOL 2. PORT FORT 3. LOGY DOGIE 4. MAVEN HAVEN 5. MARRY GARY 6. ERRANT PARENT 7. STRESSES DRESSES

1. Distant planet (1)

2. Ohio senator's backers (1)

3. Hodges' exercises (1)

4. Fire at beast (1)

5. Purple herd (1)

6. Twangy herb (2)

7. Want electrical job done again (2)

ANSWERS:
1. FAR STAR 2. GLENN MEN 3. GILS DRILLS 4. SHOOT BRUTE
5. MAUVE DROVE 6. NASAL BASIL 7. DESIRE REWIRE

1. Prohibit Peter (1)

□□□■□□□

2. Gigantic 2-man sled (1)

□□□□■□□□□

3. Battle fatigue (1)

□□□□□■□□□□□

4. Official demand for passport (2)

□□□□□□■□□□□□

5. Kevin's beer mugs (1)

□□□□□□■□□□□□□

6. Italian city's stately building (2)

□□□□■□□□□

7. Martin Luther King (2)

□□□□□□□□■□□□□□□□

ANSWERS:
1. BAN PAN 2. HUGE LUGE 3. TROOP DROOP 4. BORDER ORDER 5. KLINES STEINS 6. ROME DOME 7. PREACHER TEACHER

1. Villain movie (1)

2. Crooked copper? (1)

3. First-rate herb (1)

4. Ohio devil (2)

5. Looked for nothing (1)

6. Arlene fox-trots (2)

7. Goodness! Roomy! (2)

ANSWERS:
1. HEEL REEL 2. BENT CENT 3. PRIME THYME 4. DAYTON SATAN
5. SOUGHT NAUGHT 6. FRANCIS DANCES 7. GRACIOUS SPACIOUS

1. **Purchases cravats (1)**

2. **Crooked again (2)**

3. **Mississippi city's glue (3)**

4. **Happy with wine (2)**

5. **Snub sufficiently (2)**

6. **Ingenious connecting conveyance (2)**

7. **Low quality inside portion (4)**

ANSWERS:
1. BUYS TIES 2. ASKEW ANEW 3. BILOXI EPOXY 4. SHERRY MERRY 5. REBUFF ENOUGH 6. SUBTLE SHUTTLE 7. INFERIOR INTERIOR

1. **Dull conversation (1)**

2. **Pastry wagon (1)**

3. **Needs laugh (1)**

4. **Front steps gang (1)**

5. **Jupiter's ovens (1)**

6. **Boxer who weighs less (2)**

7. **Screamed in anger (1)**

ANSWERS:
1. DRAB GAB 2. TART CART 3. LACKS YAKS 4. STOOP GROUP 5. JOVES STOVES 6. LIGHTER FIGHTER 7. SHRIEKED PIQUED

1. **Avoid marathon (1)**

2. **TV hillbilly (1)**

3. **Wicket game, all right? (2)**

4. **Growing old angrily (2)**

5. **Spa bulletin (2)**

6. **Toe-dancing's discomfort (2)**

7. **L-a-s-r-a-e-h-e-r (3)**

ANSWERS:
1. SHUN RUN 2. TUBE RUBE 3. CROQUET OK 4. AGING RAGING 5. RESORT REPORT 6. BALLETS MALAISE 7. REHEARSAL REVERSAL

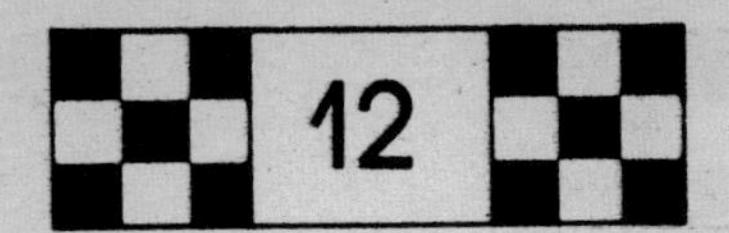

1. The Sabbath (1)

2. Criticize cartoonist Al (1)

3. Wall painting of Russian river (2)

4. Cave slogan (2)

5. Palace serf (2)

6. Poe maiden's caballeros (2)

7. Pearl's pigs (2)

ANSWERS:
1. PRAY DAY 2. RAP CAPP 3. URAL MURAL 4. GROTTO MOTTO 5. CASTLE VASSAL 6. LENORES SENORS 7. MINNIES GUINEAS

1. Holbrook's buddies (1)

2. Flimsy deck wood (1)

3. Irving hero's musical instruments (1)

4. Noisy medicine? (2)

5. Fold rental agreement (1)

6. Medical facility skeptic (2)

7. Philippine wickerwork (2)

ANSWERS:
1. HALS PALS 2. WEAK TEAK 3. GARPS HARPS 4. SONIC TONIC
5. CREASE LEASE 6. CLINIC CYNIC 7. BATAAN RATTAN

1. Possesses liveliness (1)

2. Early morn air inhalation (1)

3. Dracula's toothache? (1)

4. Trifling black eye (2)

5. Dangerous load (2)

6. Undulating Rudyard (2)

7. Turkish coin debacle (3)

ANSWERS:
1. HAS JAZZ 2. DAWN YAWN 3. FANG PANG 4. MINOR SHINER 5. HARMFUL ARMFUL 6. RIPPLING KIPLING 7. PIASTER DISASTER

1. Gloomy Othello (1)

2. Oriental eye's admirers (1)

3. Pretend soreness (1)

4. Therefore uptight (1)

5. Metallic rounded roof (1)

6. Ellery's salad (1)

7. Cut out Merlin's picture (2)

ANSWERS:
1. DOUR MOOR 2. CHANS FANS 3. FEIGN PAIN 4. HENCE TENSE
5. CHROME DOME 6. QUEENS GREENS 7. SCISSORED WIZARD

1. **Snoopy drinking vessel (1)**

2. **Diving bird's chatter (1)**

3. **Winnie's gang (1)**

4. **Jason's boat's freight (2)**

5. **Verdict for Berle? (2)**

6. **Harden English (2)**

7. **So long, fronton sport (2)**

ANSWERS:
1. PUP CUP 2. AUK TALK 3. POOH CREW 4. ARGO CARGO 5. GUILTY MILTY 6. TOUGHEN MUFFIN 7. BYEBYE JAI ALAI

1. Joke on a golf course? (1)

2. Ms. Scala, meet Ms. Farrow (2)

3. Rubies at 30 paces? (2)

4. Annoys Lone Star State (2)

5. Certain dancers' trademarks (2)

6. Bother clown (2)

7. Slow crow (2)

ANSWERS:
1. TEE HEE 2. GIA MIA 3. JEWEL DUEL 4. VEXES TEXAS
5. GOGOS LOGOS 6. PESTER JESTER 7. BACKWARD BLACKBIRD

1. **Remus rabbit's home (1)**

2. **The only "Princess" (1)**

3. **Perspiring millionaire (2)**

4. **Aviator's grommets (2)**

5. **Lessee's punishment (2)**

6. **Assembled egg pudding (2)**

7. **Author Max's sleeping cars (2)**

ANSWERS:
1. BRER LAIR 2. LONE PHONE 3. SWEATY GETTY 4. PILOTS EYELETS 5. TENANTS PENANCE 6. MUSTERED CUSTARD 7. SHULMANS PULLMANS

1. Film festival buff (1)

2. Fulfilled bridge contract (1)

3. Arnold called (1)

4. Is fond of small children (1)

5. Worldwide search (1)

6. Robin ought to (1)

7. Motioned after he did (2)

ANSWERS:
1. CANNES FAN 2. MADE SPADE 3. STANG RANG 4. LIKES TYKES
5. GLOBE PROBE 6. HOOD SHOULD 7. BECKONED SECOND

1. Make money at roulette (1)

2. Fruit skin repast (1)

3. Dial tone (1)

4. Stylish Soho cop (2)

5. Scattered shortly (1)

6. Beg for sewing tool (2)

7. Cowardly curved sword (2)

ANSWERS:
1. WIN SPIN 2. PEEL MEAL 3. PHONE DRONE 4. NOBBY BOBBY
5. STREWN SOON 6. WHEEDLE NEEDLE 7. GUTLESS CUTLASS

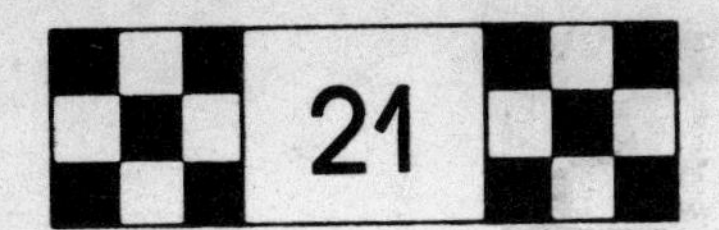

1. **Takeover of animal park (1)**

2. **Get rid of Little (1)**

3. **Reject sea bird (1)**

4. **Plowed packing a pistol (1)**

5. **Semite's beetles (2)**

6. **Hatchet thrower (2)**

7. **Porch for non-military personnel (3)**

ANSWERS:
1. ZOO COUP 2. DITCH RICH 3. SPURN TERN 4. FARMED ARMED 5. ARABS SCARABS 6. CLEAVER HEAVER 7. CIVILIAN PAVILION

1. Fetch Fido (1)

2. Short enemy (1)

3. Celery rebellion? (1)

4. Extra seat (1)

5. Stops dance (1)

6. Burned postal (1)

7. Drew closely together in confusion (2)

ANSWERS:
1. GET PET 2. LOW FOE 3. STALK BALK 4. SPARE CHAIR 5. HALTS WALTZ 6. CHARRED CARD 7. HUDDLED MUDDLED

1. Give money to Doris (1)

2. Travel suitcase (1)

3. Sam started golf game (1)

4. Bleached palm leaf (1)

5. Plie in French port (2)

6. Dog's tent-dress (2)

7. Ill at sea (2)

ANSWERS:
1. PAY DAY 2. TRIP GRIP 3. SNEAD TEED 4. BLOND FROND
5. CALAIS BALLET 6. CANINE ALINE 7. AILING SAILING

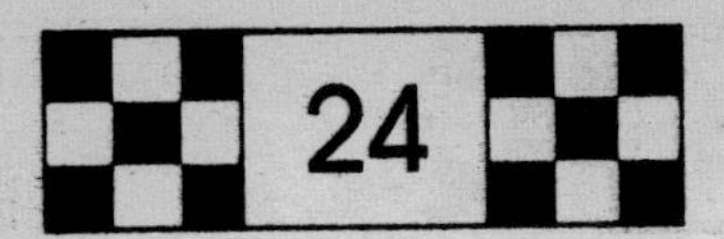

1. Swinging climbing plant (2)

2. Lubricates springs (1)

3. Russian news agency VIPs (1)

4. Gave medicine to party giver (1)

5. Track down ethnic group (1)

6. Some prisoners' coded messages (2)

7. Devilish memory aid (3)

ANSWERS:
1. JIVY IVY 2. OILS COILS 3. TASS BRASS 4. DOSED HOST
5. TRACE RACE 6. LIFERS CIPHERS 7. DEMONIC MNEMONIC

1. Single sister (1)

2. Make a lace bonnet (1)

3. Serious house plant (1)

4. Colorado ski run (1)

5. Warming of an animal's foot (1)

6. Dell on Pacific isle (2)

7. Hairy chase (2)

ANSWERS:
1. ONE NUN 2. TAT HAT 3. STERN FERN 4. VAIL TRAIL
5. PAW THAW 6. BALI VALLEY 7. HIRSUTE PURSUIT

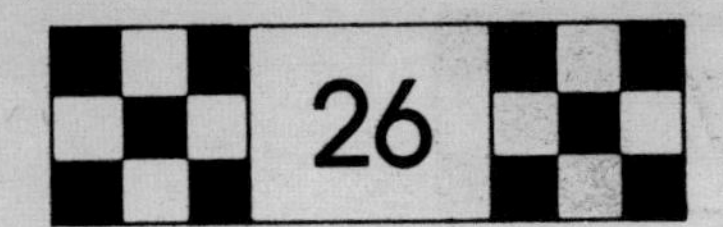

1. **Lacking caviar (1)**

2. **Gun chaps (1)**

3. **Conceited Citizen (1)**

4. **Turn around Keenan (2)**

5. **Spooky wigwam (2)**

6. **Morgan's peep shows (2)**

7. **Snowing cats and dogs? No, it's a ... (2)**

ANSWERS:
1. NO ROE 2. STEN MEN 3. VAIN KANE 4. SPIN WYNN
5. CREEPY TEPEE 6. HARRYS RAREES 7. LIZARD BLIZZARD

1. Everyone creeps (1)

2. Lizard skin (1)

3. Actor Robert's swallows (1)

4. French city traffic jam (1)

5. Swindle nephew's sister (1)

6. Sills' problems (2)

7. Marlon's pickles (2)

ANSWERS:
1. ALL CRAWL 2. NEWT SUIT 3. CULPS GULPS 4. ARLES SNARL
5. FLEECE NIECE 6. BUBBLES TROUBLES 7. PERKINS GHERKINS

1. **Mrs. Nixon's headgear (1)**

2. **Ark reptiles (2)**

3. **Hatchet strikes (1)**

4. **Carthaginian garb (2)**

5. **Grouchy Little Rascal (2)**

6. **Italian city's pastas? (2)**

7. **Baseball's Happy's P.R. men? (2)**

ANSWERS:
1. PATS HATS 2. NOAHS BOAS 3. AXE WHACKS 4. PUNIC TUNIC 5. CRANKY SPANKY 6. NAPLES STAPLES 7. CHANDLERS HANDLERS

1. Much ado about mink? (1)

2. Store of knowledge on hockey great (1)

3. Grab 40 winks (1)

4. Feel sorry for Thurber's Walter (2)

5. Non-metallic element, imbecile (2)

6. Ruins eyeglasses (1)

7. Cuban plain (3)

ANSWERS:
1. FUR STIR 2. ORR LORE 3. SEIZE ZS 4. PITY MITTY
5. BORON MORON 6. WRECKS SPECS 7. HAVANA SAVANNA

1. More faithful cow (2)

2. Engine lugger (2)

3. Pear-shaped Muslim temple? (1)

4. Traps grizzlies (1)

5. Last-mentioned subject (2)

6. Lilly's gliding motions (2)

7. Pia's hats (3)

ANSWERS:
1. TRUER MOOER 2. MOTOR TOTER 3. BOSC MOSQUE 4. SNARES BEARS
5. LATTER MATTER 6. DACHES SASHAYS 7. ZADORAS FEDORAS

1. **Embrace the big guy (1)**

2. **Give a young lady a smooch (1)**

3. **Valentine greeting writer (1)**

4. **Honest desire (1)**

5. **Be crazy about love (2)**

6. **Chocolates? Great! (2)**

7. **Greek confection (1)**

ANSWERS:
1. HUG LUG 2. KISS MISS 3. CARD BARD 4. JUST LUST
5. ADORE AMOR 6. CANDY DANDY 7. CRETE SWEET

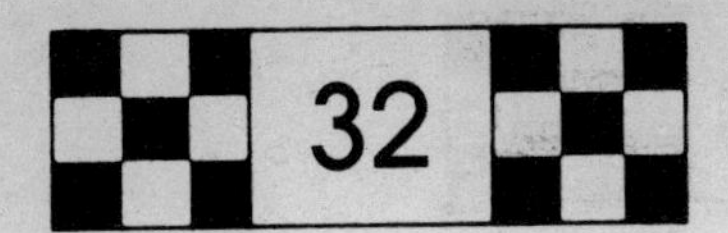

1. Eczema caused by meat mixture (1)

2. Very important Venetian's opera boxes (2)

3. Hot memoirs (3)

4. Prettier when more scantily clad (2)

5. Observer of waste conduit (2)

6. Cosell bathed (2)

7. Fodder decaying (2)

ANSWERS:
1. HASH RASH 2. DOGES LOGES 3. FIERY DIARY 4. FAIRER BARER
5. SEWER VIEWER 6. HOWARD SHOWERED 7. SOILAGE SPOILAGE

1. Denim display (1)

2. Funny spicy bean dish (2)

3. Keyed up Hamlin musician (2)

4. A world of townhouses? (2)

5. Embarrass Indian fighting general (2)

6. Relax, pussycat (2)

7. Eternal dieting (2)

ANSWERS:
1. JEAN SCENE 2. SILLY CHILI 3. HYPER PIPER 4. MONDO CONDO
5. FLUSTER CUSTER 6. RECLINE FELINE 7. LASTING FASTING

1. Appointment to shred? (1)

2. Confederate elf (2)

3. Coarse pretense (1)

4. Tidier Pan (2)

5. Rented vicious dog (1)

6. Used forensics joyfully (3)

7. Catastrophic vinyl (2)

ANSWERS
1. GRATE DATE 2. DIXIE PIXIE 3. ROUGH BLUFF 4. NEATER PETER 5. LEASED BEAST 6. DEBATED ELATED 7. DRASTIC PLASTIC

1. Running in wooden shoes (1)

2. Wove a double entendre (1)

3. Jump over certain tide (1)

4. Capp family nonsense (2)

5. Misrepresent answer (2)

6. Taste enthusiast (2)

7. Shiny-coated classic car (2)

ANSWERS:
1. CLOG JOG 2. SPUN PUN 3. LEAP NEAP 4. YOKUM HOKUM
5. BELIE REPLY 6. FLAVOR RAVER 7. LACQUERED PACKARD

1. Olympic medals for Phil and Steve (1)

2. Majors' snow shoes (1)

3. U.S. athletes' vision of gold (1)

4. Rough ice competition for goals (2)

5. Judging an ice event (2)

6. Twirling skater who is medalist (2)

7. Speed skater in February Olympics (2)

ANSWERS:
1. TWIN WIN 2. LEES SKIS 3. TEAM DREAM 4. ROCKY HOCKEY
5. RATING SKATING 6. SPINNER WINNER 7. WINTER SPRINTER

1. Put Dunaway on a scale (1)

2. Drop slop (1)

3. German city's businesses (1)

4. Grouchy in the morning (2)

5. Meek antique (2)

6. Bird's biscuits (2)

7. Clergy's raincoats (2)

ANSWERS:
1. WEIGH FAYE 2. SPILL SWILL 3. WORMS FIRMS 4. SURLY EARLY
5. DOCILE FOSSIL 6. PUFFINS MUFFINS 7. VICARS SLICKERS

1. **B. Ross's sewing kit? (1)**

2. **Franklin's desires (1)**

3. **Make metal statue of Washington (1)**

4. **Cease fire (2)**

5. **Mrs. John and Mrs. John Quincy (2)**

6. **Young Washington's confessions (1)**

7. **Pudding n' pie (2)**

ANSWERS:
1. FLAG BAG 2. BENS YENS 3. FORGE GEORGE 4. STIFLE RIFLE
5. ADAMS MADAMS 6. YOUTHS TRUTHS 7. GEORGIE PORGIE

1. Speech by one who wants war (1)

2. Bracelet ornament (1)

3. Drive out indecision (1)

4. DDE's preferences (1)

5. Fibbers' hair blowers (2)

6. Sardonic $6,000,000 man (3)

7. Subterranean pub (2)

ANSWERS:
1. HAWK TALK 2. ARM CHARM 3. ROUT DOUBT 4. IKES LIKES
5. LIARS DRYERS 6. IRONIC BIONIC 7. CAVERN TAVERN

1. **Concealed tot (1)**

2. **How body builders increase collar size (1)**

3. **Pictured lying down (1)**

4. **Kidnapped punctuation mark (2)**

5. **Less adept oarsman (2)**

6. **Castle of evil (2)**

7. **Drank greedily, in confusion (2)**

ANSWERS:
1. HID KID 2. FLEX NECKS 3. SHOWN PRONE 4. STOLEN COLON 5. SLOWER ROWER 6. MALICE PALACE 7. GUZZLED PUZZLED

1. **Agile fellow (1)**

2. **Referring to Scotch lass's speech (1)**

3. **Without nasal passage (2)**

4. **Archibald's salary requirements (1)**

5. **Valerie Harper's beverages (2)**

6. **Pancake sparkle (2)**

7. **Fire-eater's bottles for wine (2)**

ANSWERS:
1. SPRY GUY 2. HER BURR 3. MINUS SINUS 4. NATES RATES 5. RHODAS SODAS 6. FRITTER GLITTER 7. DRAGONS FLAGONS

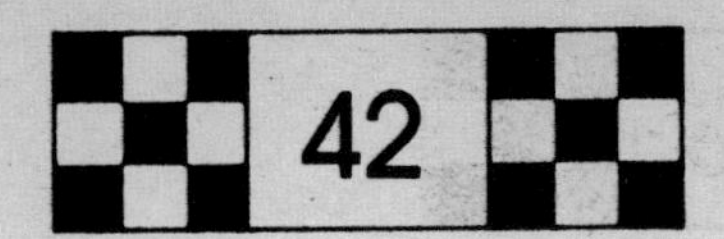

1. **Boring bird (1)**

2. **Males in today's winner's family (1)**

3. **Person doing a lube job (2)**

4. **The fire was no accident, Johnny (2)**

5. **Ingalls' distinctive airs (2)**

6. **Abhor entreaty (2)**

7. **Calumniates Abby's twin (2)**

ANSWERS:
1. DULL GULL 2. WRENN MEN 3. OILER TOILER 4. ARSON CARSON
5. LAURAS AURAS 6. DETEST REQUEST 7. SLANDERS LANDERS

1. Closed shack (1)

2. Miss Jackson's dishes (1)

3. Wine cake (1)

4. Junior's cash (2)

5. Farmer playing on N.Y. hockey team? (2)

6. One with hunger for artistic pursuits (2)

7. Craftsman supporting a cause (3)

ANSWERS:
1. SHUT HUT 2. KATES PLATES 3. PORT TORTE 4. SONNYS MONIES
5. GRANGER RANGER 6. CULTURE VULTURE 7. PARTISAN ARTISAN

1. **Japanese sash for desert wear (2)**

2. **Formally observe this day (1)**

3. **Almost a lascivious look (1)**

4. **Sassy radar signal (1)**

5. **Pigtails (1)**

6. **Austrian composer's home (1)**

7. **Operation lied about under oath (3)**

ANSWERS:
1. GOBI OBI 2. KEEP LEAP 3. NEAR LEER 4. FLIP BLIP 5. HAIR PAIR 6. STRAUSS HOUSE 7. SURGERY PERJURY

1. Cherrystone preserve (1)

☐☐☐☐■☐☐☐

2. Dawber's hats (1)

☐☐☐☐■☐☐☐☐

3. Hungry frame of mind (1)

☐☐☐☐■☐☐☐☐

4. Acorn's grandparents? (1)

☐☐☐☐■☐☐☐☐☐

5. Leased false teeth? (2)

☐☐☐☐☐☐■☐☐☐☐☐☐

6. Sink passenger conveyance (2)

☐☐☐☐☐☐☐■☐☐☐☐☐☐☐

7. Whale washer (2)

☐☐☐☐☐☐☐■☐☐☐☐☐☐☐☐

ANSWERS:
1. CLAM JAM 2. PAMS TAMS 3. FOOD MOOD 4. OAKS FOLKS
5. DENTAL RENTAL 5. SCUTTLE SHUTTLE 7. BLUBBER SCRUBBER

1. **Pretty good wine (2)**

2. **Hops drying in kiln (1)**

3. **Tobacco pipe purchaser (2)**

4. **Taste preserver (2)**

5. **Eye condition from small type (1)**

6. **Auction joker (2)**

7. **Loot town (2)**

ANSWERS:
1. OK TOKAY 2. OAST ROAST 3. BRIAR BUYER 4. FLAVOR SAVER 5. PRINT SQUINT 6. BIDDER KIDDER 7. PILLAGE VILLAGE

1. Way to imitate Van Gogh (1)

2. Fried egg calamity (1)

3. Bend carpus (1)

4. Hod man, Robards (2)

5. TV cook's ladles (2)

6. Shish kebabed waiter (2)

7. How pig finds fungi (2)

ANSWERS:
1. SHEAR EAR 2. YOLK BROKE 3. TWIST WRIST 4. MASON JASON 5. TRIPPERS DIPPERS 6. SKEWERED STEWARD 7. SNUFFLES TRUFFLES

1. Cautious Mrs. Lincoln (2)

2. Robert, Edward, Willie and Tad (1)

3. Clothes worn by infamous Dr. (1)

4. Ulysses won't (1)

5. Voice of the confederacy (1)

6. Abe is grateful to mother (1)

7. Abe ponderin' (2)

ANSWERS:
1. WARY MARY 2. ABES BABES 3. MUDDS DUDS 4. GRANT CANT 5. SOUTH MOUTH 6. THANKS HANKS 7. LINCOLN THINKIN'

1. **Unhappy buddy (1)**

2. **Faint in a while (1)**

3. **Insipid product (1)**

4. **Andropov's tantrums (2)**

5. **Macho sailor (2)**

6. **One searching for lab utensil (2)**

7. **Coaxing a young plant (2)**

ANSWERS:
1. GLUM CHUM 2. SWOON SOON 3. BLAND BRAND 4. YURI'S FURIES 5. HE-MAN SEAMAN 6. BEAKER SEEKER 7. WHEEDLING SEEDLING

1. Queer fish (1)

2. Nude successor (1)

3. Big freight vessel (1)

4. Indispensable appellation (2)

5. Rub out highest class (2)

6. Plain cheek depression (2)

7. Tolerates clumsy person (2)

ANSWERS:
1. ODD COD 2. BARE HEIR 3. LARGE BARGE 4. VITAL TITLE
5. DELETE ELITE 6. SIMPLE DIMPLE 7. STOMACHS LUMMOX

1. **Sketched a pair (1)**

2. **Diminutive musician Williams (1)**

3. **Referred to season starting today (1)**

4. **Bloody honor (2)**

5. **Conclusion about to take place (2)**

6. **Mack-of-the-movies' doctrines (2)**

7. **Travels around selling foot levers (2)**

ANSWERS:
1. DREW TWO 2. SMALL PAUL 3. MEANT LENT 4. GORY GLORY
5. ENDING PENDING 6. SENNETT'S TENETS 7. PEDDLES TREADLES

1. **Cut down all the corn (1)**

2. **Sand bar burrower (1)**

3. **Connery's little deer (1)**

4. **Kept out comedian (1)**

5. **More sensible Mitzi (2)**

6. **Marx Brother's teas (2)**

7. **Chinese soup in jai alai arena (2)**

ANSWERS:
1. CHOP CROP 2. SHOAL MOLE 3. SEAN'S FAWNS 4. BARRED CARD
5. SANER GAYNOR 6. CHICO'S PEKOES 7. FRONTON WONTON

1. Worn out part of shoe (1)

2. Proper person without clothes (1)

3. Amos' lascivious partner? (2)

4. Agile band instrument (2)

5. One on a snap-eating spree (2)

6. What Rosie does to hedges? (2)

7. Feeling caused by loss of rank (3)

ANSWERS:
1. SOLE HOLE 2. NUDE PRUDE 3. RANDY ANDY 4. NIMBLE CYMBAL 5. GINGER BINGER 6. RIVETS PRIVETS 7. DEMOTION EMOTION

1. **World-ending explosion (1)**

2. **Leading man's limousines (1)**

3. **Leonard's lures (2)**

4. **One signboard (2)**

5. **Overjoyed when anesthetized (3)**

6. **Car rug plan (2)**

7. **Park birds' crumbs (2)**

ANSWERS:
1. DOOM BOOM 2. STAR'S CARS 3. NIMOY'S DECOYS 4. SINGLE SHINGLE 5. ELATED SEDATED 6. FLOORMAT FORMAT 7. PIGEONS' SMIDGENS

1. Fly society (1)

2. Jungle king's charged atoms (2)

3. Cornered Donna (1)

4. Gnomes' dirigibles (1)

5. Smooth Italian (2)

6. Snugger ecclesiastical headdress (2)

7. Flaming desire (2)

ANSWERS:
1. GNAT FRAT 2. LIONS IONS 3. TREED REED 4. IMPS' BLIMPS
5. SATIN LATIN 6. TIGHTER MITRE 7. BURNING YEARNING

1. **Overconfident boxer (1)**

2. **Mooch shield (1)**

3. **Unexpected quick look (1)**

4. **Actor Gert's searches (1)**

5. **J.R.'s family's activities (2)**

6. **Reject artwork (2)**

7. **Spreads news of batter cake (2)**

ANSWERS:
1. SMUG PUG 2. CADGE BADGE 3. CHANCE GLANCE 4. FROBE'S PROBES 5. EWING'S DOINGS 6. DECLINE DESIGN 7. TRUMPETS CRUMPETS

1. Auto body repairman (1)

2. Not the tune requested (1)

3. Pinch part of face (1)

4. Send back an order (2)

5. Pamper actor Lou (2)

6. Thinner maid (2)

7. Oarsman's donuts (2)

ANSWERS:
1. DENT GENT 2. WRONG SONG 3. TWEAK CHEEK 4. REMAND DEMAND 5. COSSET GOSSETT 6. LEANER CLEANER 7. SCULLER'S CRULLERS

1. Place of Dracula's mark (1)

2. Free from possibility of error (1)

3. Winnie's evidence (1)

4. Slipping self-esteem (1)

5. Be sorry about a happening (2)

6. Today's implacable winner (2)

7. Placido's exotic birds (3)

ANSWERS:
1. BITE SITE 2. GOOF PROOF 3. POOH'S CLUES 4. PRIDE SLIDE
5. REPENT EVENT 6. DEADPAN BEDYAN 7. DOMINGO'S FLAMINGOS

1. **String up the whole passel! (1)**

2. **Perspiring Satchmo (2)**

3. **Less risky biscuit (2)**

4. **String band gent (2)**

5. **Perfume affair (2)**

6. **Quick look from parsonage (1)**

7. **Smelled talent (1)**

ANSWERS:
1. HANG GANG 2. DEWY LOUIS 3. SAFER WAFER 4. CELLO FELLOW
5. ATTAR MATTER 6. MANSE GLANCE 7. SNIFFED GIFT

1. He's no angel! (1)

2. Deceptive move by Patrick (1)

3. Faded picture of today's namesake? (1)

4. Color him green! (1)

5. Sully name of Patrick? (1)

6. Patrick's lament (1)

7. Oddly picturesque Patrick (1)

ANSWERS:
1. AINT SAINT 2. SAINT FEINT 3. FAINT SAINT 4. PAINT SAINT
5. TAINT SAINT 6. SAINT PLAINT 7. QUAINT SAINT

1. **When a trick makes headlines, it's... (1)**

2. **Is fond of certain fish (1)**

3. **Tosses peaches (1)**

4. **Bare-headed sky bearer (2)**

5. **Make up a purpose (2)**

6. **Joy notwithstanding (2)**

7. **Tittering while squirming (2)**

ANSWERS:
1. RUSE NEWS 2. LIKES PIKES 3. FLINGS CLINGS 4. HATLESS ATLAS
5. INVENT INTENT 6. DESPITE DELIGHT 7. GIGGLING WIGGLING

1. Tastes potatoes (1)

2. Insane sudden fear (2)

3. Turn in badge (1)

4. Dog kiss (1)

5. Hope's nasal tones (1)

6. Actor Richards' sidewalk scams (2)

7. Soho cop's avocations (2)

ANSWERS:
1. TRIES FRIES 2. MANIC PANIC 3. YIELD SHIELD 4. POOCH SMOOCH 5. LANCE'S TWANGS 6. CONTE'S MONTES 7. BOBBY'S HOBBIES

1. What is the reason for tears? (1)

2. Onion-like odor (1)

3. Uneven written matter (2)

4. Accumulates lumber (1)

5. Ardent maid (2)

6. Tinier wood carver (2)

7. Squirming giving up 10% (2)

ANSWERS:
1. WHY CRY 2. LEEK REEK 3. CHOPPY COPY 4. HOARDS BOARDS
5. FERVENT SERVANT 6. LITTLER WHITTLER 7. WRITHING TITHING

1. Was aware of thaw (1)

2. Adorable little sprout (1)

3. Seasonal songfest (1)

4. Place for early spring flower (2)

5. Fear of snowfall

6. Gratifyin' time of year (2)

7. Fish doctor (2)

ANSWERS:
1. FELT MELT 2. CUTE SHOOT 3. SPRING SING 4. CROCUS LOCUS 5. FLURRY WORRY 6. PLEASIN' SEASON 7. STURGEON SURGEON

1. **Trophy case (1)**

2. **Illegal gambling on hockey is an ... (1)**

3. **Makes commotion in penalty area (1)**

4. **Making a hockey goal by chance (1)**

5. **Make another goal! (1)**

6. **Perforated keeper (2)**

7. **Babbling while on the ice (2)**

ANSWERS:
1. WIN BIN 2. ICE VICE 3. ROCKS BOX 4. PUCK LUCK
5. SCORE MORE 6. HOLEY GOALIE 7. SKATING PRATING

1. Mailed house payment (1)

2. Listens to phobias (1)

3. Strange question (2)

4. Interval of relief from tyrant (2)

5. St. Valentine's Day massacre (2)

6. Blocks ashes (2)

7. Decisive confrontation in Detroit (2)

ANSWERS:
1. SENT RENT 2. HEARS FEARS 3. EERIE QUERY 4. DESPOT RESPITE 5. GARAGE BARRAGE 6. HINDERS CINDERS 7. MOTOWN SHOWDOWN

1. **Giant step (1)**

2. **S.A. monkey's pastas (2)**

3. **Elixir for ancient priest (2)**

4. **Stringed instrument's notes (1)**

5. **More mature solderer (2)**

6. **Customer's knowledge (2)**

7. **One-legged buying spree? (2)**

ANSWERS:
1. WIDE STRIDE 2. TITIS ZITIS 3. DRUID FLUID 4. HARP'S SHARPS 5. ELDER WELDER 6. CLIENT'S SCIENCE 7. HOPPING SHOPPING

1. Stallone's questions (1)

2. Prepare Nelson (2)

3. Excellent string (1)

4. Which one's opinions? (1)

5. Study Jules (1)

6. Silly Annapolis man (2)

7. Craziest one who enjoys being cruel (2)

ANSWERS:
1. SLY'S WHYS 2. READY EDDY 3. FINE TWINE 4. WHOSE VIEWS 5. LEARN VERNE 6. GIDDY MIDDY 7. MADDEST SADIST

1. Lass went to church (1)

2. Bee colony's married ladies (1)

3. Cries a lot (1)

4. Consumes candy and cake (1)

5. Twists objects (1)

6. Tussle on railroad bridge (2)

7. Watch an exercise class (2)

ANSWERS:
1. MAID PRAYED 2. HIVE'S WIVES 3. WEEPS HEAPS 4. EATS SWEETS
5. WRINGS THINGS 6. TRESTLE WRESTLE 7. WITNESS FITNESS

1. Read top line of eye chart (1)

2. Which person's church seats? (1)

3. Tower made of stockings? (2)

4. Sun hat (2)

5. Fear of making a mistake (2)

6. Well-known detective (2)

7. Mr. Majors' urgent requests (1)

ANSWERS:
1. SEE E 2. WHO'S PEWS 3. NYLON PYLON 4. SOLAR BOWLER
5. ERROR TERROR 6. FAMOUS SHAMUS 7. LEE'S PLEAS

1. Follow Moby Dick! (1)

2. The duck has laryngitis. It ... (1)

3. Mail vandal? (2)

4. Looking for John's Society (1)

5. Covers corridor floors (1)

6. Sondheim, yet (2)

7. Odd stringed instrument (2)

ANSWERS:
1. TAIL WHALE 2. LACKS QUACKS 3. ARMOR HARMER 4. BIRCH SEARCH 5. TILES AISLES 6. STEPHEN EVEN 7. BIZARRE GUITAR

1. Get maple syrup (1)

2. Makes church windows (1)

3. Pure garbage (1)

4. March leaving like a lion (2)

5. Veterans' area (2)

6. Spot for a lamenter (2)

7. Debra's look-alikes (2)

ANSWERS:
1. TAP SAP 2. STAINS PANES 3. CHASTE WASTE 4. GOING BLOWING 5. LEGION REGION 6. MOURNER CORNER 7. WINGER'S RINGERS

1. Lunch whistle (1)

2. Sudden desire for sacred song (1)

3. Basketball or tennis is a ... (1)

4. Sarcastic electronic man (3)

5. Author Louis' books' attraction (2)

6. Stefanie's baths (2)

7. Norman's greeters (2)

ANSWERS:
1. NOON TUNE 2. HYMN WHIM 3. COURT SPORT 4. IRONIC BIONIC
5. LAMOUR ALLURE 6. POWERS SHOWERS 7. MAILERS HAILERS

1. Short haircut (1)
2. Buzz Bo
3. Base awarded for pitcher error (1)
4. Old folks were incensed (1)
5. One who takes fibbing to new peaks (2)
6. Relatives? Loads ! (2)
7. Certain pigeons' obstacles (3)

ANSWERS:
1. BOB JOB 2. BEEP PEEP 3. BALK WALK 4. AGED RAGED
5. HIGHER LIAR 6. COUSINS DOZENS 7. CARRIERS BARRIERS

1. Pleads for breakfast (1)

2. Egyptian novice (2)

3. Used car salesman's pitch (1)

4. Port-au-Prince, sailor (2)

5. Grab the American! (1)

6. Actor William's a,e,i,o,u (2)

7. Scotland's Skye is a ... (2)

ANSWERS:
1. BEGS EGGS 2. CAIRO TYRO 3. WHEEL SPIEL 4. HAITI MATEY 5. SEIZE CHEESE 6. POWELLS VOWELS 7. HIGHLAND ISLAND

1. Paymaster's cubicle (1)

2. Big cat from Arizona town (2)

3. London park tour director (1)

4. Motorless plane occupant (2)

5. Locked door, took a nap (1)

6. Fix the ceiling more quickly! (2)

7. Rejecting salary (2)

ANSWERS:
1. WAGE CAGE 2. YUMA PUMA 3. HYDE GUIDE 4. GLIDER RIDER 5. CLOSED DOZED 6. PLASTER FASTER 7. SPURNING EARNING

1. Solid fat (1)

2. More recent achiever (2)

3. Domino's footwear (1)

4. Norman's watery eyes (1)

5. Check M or F (2)

6. Terrible news (2)

7. NFL commissioner's wines (2)

ANSWERS:
1. HARD LARD 2. NEWER DOER 3. FATS SPATS 4. LEARS TEARS
5. RENDER GENDER 6. FEARFUL EARFUL 7. ROZELLES MOSELLES

1. **Breezy speedway (2)**

2. **Shook up Shakespeare (1)**

3. **Flowery lesson (2)**

4. **Devil of a sailor! (2)**

5. **Socks and stockings are ... (1)**

6. **Stocks up on weapons (1)**

7. **Confuse famous Indian fighter (2)**

ANSWERS:
1. WINDY INDY 2. JARRED BARD 3. FLORAL MORAL 4. DEMON SEAMAN 5. TOES CLOTHES 6. HOARDS SWORDS 7. FLUSTER CUSTER

1. **High class horse (2)**

2. **Fellow's height (1)**

3. **Land grabber (2)**

4. **Get Francis or Roger up (2)**

5. **Censure self-importance (1)**

6. **More subservient klutz (2)**

7. **Before hair started to go (3)**

ANSWERS:
1. TONY PONY 2. GUYS SIZE 3. ACRE TAKER 4. WAKEN BACON 5. CHIDE PRIDE 6. HUMBLER BUMBLER 7. PRECEDING RECEDING

1. **Miss Saint's prima donnas (2)**

2. **Flatten Satan (2)**

3. **Lesson for horn players (1)**

4. **Heavenly pattern (2)**

5. **Insurgents' stones (2)**

6. **Awe induced by mistake (2)**

7. **Driver's shoes (2)**

ANSWERS:
1. EVAS DIVAS 2. LEVEL DEVIL 3. BRASS CLASS 4. DIVINE DESIGN
5. REBELS PEBBLES 6. BLUNDER WONDER 7. CHAUFFEURS LOAFERS

1. Run away, little horse! (1)

2. Result of prolonged hitchhiking? (1)

3. Loud, overbearing sheep (2)

4. Out of the mouths of babes come... (1)

5. Soft "touch" (2)

6. Hand-to-hand fight in place of worship (2)

7. Exiting unsteadily (2)

ANSWERS:
1. BOLT COLT 2. NUMB THUMB 3. WOOLLY BULLY 4. YOUTHS TRUTHS 5. TENDER LENDER 6. CHAPEL GRAPPLE 7. LEAVING WEAVING

1. Frost on citrus fruit (1)

2. Unfettered Greek deity (1)

3. Vessel's radar signals (1)

4. Fat dog (1)

5. Guard at the gate (2)

6. Power's twisters (2)

7. Slipshod when bald (2)

ANSWERS:
1. LIME RIME 2. LOOSE ZEUS 3. SHIPS BLIPS 4. ROUND HOUND
5. ENTRY SENTRY 6. TYRONES CYCLONES 7. CARELESS HAIRLESS

1. Possessed nail (1)

2. Nanny's cereal (1)

3. Rah-rahs from stadium seats (1)

4. Make certain of irresistibility (2)

5. Rewrite death scene (2)

6. Trembling while screeching to a halt (2)

7. Doodling brother or sister (2)

ANSWERS:
1. HAD BRAD 2. GOATS OATS 3. TIERS CHEERS 4. ASSURE ALLURE
5. REVISE DEMISE 6. SHAKING BRAKING 7. SCRIBBLING SIBLING

1. Surcharge on floor product (1)

2. Get payment from Attila (1)

3. They got Astaire's last penny (1)

4. Certain Uncle's "stings" (1)

5. Tax on freight vessel (1)

6. Angrier tax totaler (2)

7. Tenant's 1040 form (3)

ANSWERS:
1. WAX TAX 2. DUN HUN 3. BLED FRED 4. SAMS SCAMS
5. BARGE CHARGE 6. MADDER ADDER 7. OCCUPANT DOCUMENT

1. Tune that's an Oscar contender (1)

2. Oscar is on the vessel (2)

3. Kevin's script (1)

4. First-to-arrive MacLaine (2)

5. Person escorting Debra (2)

6. Allen's yummies (2)

7. Hemingway's antennae (3)

ANSWERS:
1. STRONG SONG 2. AWARD ABOARD 3. KLINES LINES 4. EARLY SHIRLEY 5. WINGER BRINGER 6. WOODYS GOODIES 7. MARIELS AERIALS

1. That girl's disparaging comment (1)

2. Large pile of debts (1)

3. Employ one's father (1)

4. Ermine wrap (1)

5. Thin Man's neck spasms (1)

6. Worthless five iron (2)

7. Guess it was a shock (2)

ANSWERS:
1. HER SLUR 2. BILL HILL 3. HIRE SIRE 4. STOAT COAT
5. NICKS CRICKS 6. TRASHY MASHIE 7. SURMISE SURPRISE

1. Certain fish dinner (1)

2. $1000 orchestra (1)

3. Parents' funny remarks (1)

4. Swap pigtail (1)

5. Statistics on rock layers (2)

6. Noontime squeeze (1)

7. Suggested that body was buried (2)

ANSWERS:
1. EEL MEAL 2. GRAND BAND 3. FOLKS JOKES 4. TRADE BRAID
5. STRATA DATA 6. LUNCH CRUNCH 7. INFERRED INTERRED

1. Estimate how old someone is (1)

2. Cheap whiskey for space creature (2)

3. Mild Streisand character (2)

4. Indicate $100 bill (2)

5. Big strong dame (2)

6. Performing CIA mission in the air (2)

7. Nassau night clothes (3)

ANSWERS:
1. GAUGE AGE 2. JEDI REDEYE 3. GENTLE YENTL 4. DENOTE CNOTE
5. BURLY GIRLIE 6. FLYING SPYING 7. BAHAMAS PAJAMAS

1. Put under R for River (1)

2. Praise deception (1)

3. Actor George chortled (1)

4. Come in, wise counselor (2)

5. Create a purpose (2)

6. Decorative aid for the deaf (2)

7. High caliber sidewalk game (2)

ANSWERS:
1. FILE NILE 2. LAUD FRAUD 3. RAFT LAUGHED 4. ENTER MENTOR
5. INVENT INTENT 6. HEARING EARRING 7. TOPNOTCH HOPSCOTCH

1. Purchase egg colors (1)

2. Part of chick emerging from shell? (1)

3. Cheerful rabbit (2)

4. Brave little water bird (2)

5. One who ponders egg tints (2)

6. One who eats sumptuously tomorrow (2)

7. Candy containers' rubber rings (2)

ANSWERS:
1. BUY DYE 2. EGG LEG 3. SUNNY BUNNY 4. PLUCKY DUCKY
5. COLOR MULLER 6. EASTER FEASTER 7. BASKETS GASKETS

1. Look for onion-like plant (1)

2. Titillate veggies (1)

3. Upper class zucchini (1)

4. Paul's creamed dish (2)

5. Work havoc on slaw (2)

6. Vegetables grown in attic (3)

7. Don't overdo the green garnish. Use... (2)

ANSWERS:
1. SEEK LEEK 2. TEASE PEAS 3. POSH SQUASH 4. BUNYANS ONIONS
5. RAVAGE CABBAGE 6. GARRETS CARROTS 7. PARSLEY SPARSELY

1. Male duck decoy (1)

2. Made thief's bones rattle (1)

3. Cornel's offspring (1)

4. Get there in one piece (2)

5. More recent volcanic evidence (2)

6. One who smooches in the moonlight (2)

7. Makes fun of facial marks (2)

ANSWERS:
1. FAKE DRAKE 2. SHOOK CROOK 3. WILDE CHILD 4. ARRIVE ALIVE 5. LATER CRATER 6. LUNAR SPOONER 7. HECKLES FRECKLES

1. **Equal rights for infants? (1)**

2. **Chuckle from little cow (1)**

3. **Participants in air show (1)**

4. **Fellow's forgetfulness (1)**

5. **One learning to take bets (2)**

6. **Former Interior Secretary's collars (2)**

7. **Clothes predator (2)**

ANSWERS:
1. CRIB LIB 2. CALF LAUGH 3. LOOP GROUP 4. CHAPS LAPSE 5. ROOKIE BOOKIE 6. ICKES DICKIES 7. GARMENT VARMINT

1. Ficus branch (1)

2. N.Y. borough's traffic sounds (1)

3. Brash Stallone character (2)

4. Mental condition at roundup (2)

5. Ms. Picasso's perfumes (3)

6. Entrance laughter (2)

7. Caution, pupils (2)

ANSWERS:
1. FIG TWIG 2. BRONX HONKS 3. COCKY ROCKY 4. CORRAL MORALE 5. PALOMAS AROMAS 6. PORTAL CHORTLE 7. PRUDENCE STUDENTS

1. Noise at family reunion (1)

2. Bridge blueprint (1)

3. Easy-going chemical compound (2)

4. Coloring utensil for fabric (2)

5. Reply to the ballerina (2)

6. One who leases Rockefeller complex (2)

7. Ms. Goodman's sycophants (2)

ANSWERS:
1. KIN DIN 2. SPAN PLAN 3. PLACID ACID 4. RAYON CRAYON
5. ANSWER DANCER 6. CENTER RENTER 7. DODYS TOADIES

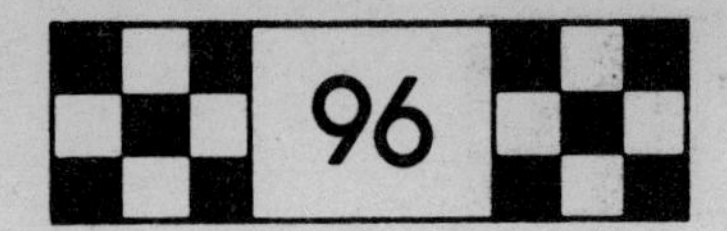

1. **Sketch face bone (1)**

2. **Regain sanity (1)**

3. **Rise in illegal activity (1)**

4. **GBS's defects (1)**

5. **Pungent sled dog (2)**

6. **Graceful bow on volcanic isle (2)**

7. **EMT bringing a litter is a ... (2)**

ANSWERS:
1. DRAW JAW 2. FIND MIND 3. CRIME CLIMB 4. SHAWS FLAWS 5. MUSKY HUSKY 6. SURTSEY CURTSY 7. STRETCHER FETCHER

1. **Expo Pete's socks (1)**

2. **Small hits by small ballplayers (1)**

3. **Peewee's sibling's daughters (2)**

4. **Dropped every ball (1)**

5. **Eccentric old Los Angeles player (2)**

6. **Play shortstop, Yankee Dave (2)**

7. **Strawberry's containers (2)**

ANSWERS:
1. ROSE HOSE 2. RUNTS BUNTS 3. REESES NIECES 4. CAUGHT NAUGHT 5. DODGER CODGER 6. INFIELD WINFIELD 7. DARRYLS BARRELS

1. Forms vases on pottery wheel (1)

2. More unusual kitchen gadget (2)

3. Astronaut senator's desires (1)

4. Culpability grew (1)

5. Coughing while inhaling (2)

6. Cartoon dog's plump dolls (2)

7. Calmer manner (3)

ANSWERS:
1. TURNS URNS 2. RARER PARER 3. GLENNS YENS 4. GUILT BUILT 5. CHOKING SMOKING 6. SNOOPYS KEWPIES 7. SERENER DEMEANOR

1. Record of running trips (1)

☐☐☐ ■ ☐☐☐

2. Rants on and on (2)

☐☐☐☐☐ ■ ☐☐☐☐

3. "Candid Camera" searches (1)

☐☐☐☐☐ ■ ☐☐☐☐☐

4. Tested self-esteem (1)

☐☐☐☐☐ ■ ☐☐☐☐☐

5. Odd ball (1)

☐☐☐☐☐ ■ ☐☐☐☐☐☐

6. More sugary liquid quart (2)

☐☐☐☐☐☐☐ ■ ☐☐☐☐☐

7. Vocalist Smith's bike tricks (2)

☐☐☐☐☐☐ ■ ☐☐☐☐☐☐☐☐

ANSWERS:
1. JOG LOG 2. RAGES AGES 3. FUNTS HUNTS 4. TRIED PRIDE
5. QUEER SPHERE 6. SWEETER LITER 7. KEELYS WHEELIES

1. Attila's jollies (1)

2. Regain sanity (1)

3. Precipitation decline (1)

4. Delicious type of pudding (2)

5. Serious ski race (2)

6. First-rate veteran actor (2)

7. Ruby in supplicating position (2)

ANSWERS:
1. HUN FUN 2. FIND MIND 3. RAIN WANE 4. TASTY HASTY
5. SOLEMN SLALOM 6. SUPER TROUPER 7. KNEELER KEELER

1. Calamari, Caesar (1)

2. Church cat (2)

3. Platter for Hall of Famer Frankie (1)

4. Wealthy actress Elaine (1)

5. Prague people's long journeys (1)

6. Charles, meet Van (2)

7. Leatherneck's whalebones (2)

ANSWERS:
1. SQUID SID 2. ABBEY TABBY 3. FRISCH DISH 4. RICH STRITCH
5. CZECHS TREKS 6. BRONSON JOHNSON 7. MARINES BALEENS

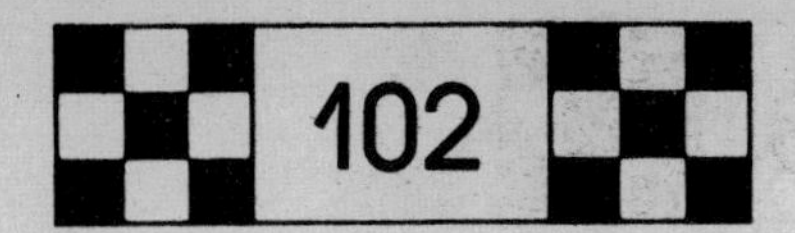

1. Fish nap (1)

2. Exude sticky substances (1)

3. Land grabber (2)

4. Tightened corset strings (1)

5. Cause formal argumentation (2)

6. Congressional body's beliefs (2)

7. Sick fowl (2)

ANSWERS:
1. COD NOD 2. OOZE GOOS 3. ACRE TAKER 4. LACED WAIST
5. CREATE DEBATE 6. SENATES TENETS 7. STRICKEN CHICKEN

1. Raised coniferous shrub (1)

2. Is unable to set seeds in ground (1)

3. Waters flowers (2)

4. Pullin' crab grass from Paradise (2)

5. Flower shop in the woods (2)

6. Eve's flower beds (2)

7. Flirt's small flower clusters (2)

ANSWERS:
1. GREW YEW 2. CANT PLANT 3. HOSES ROSES 4. WEEDIN EDEN 5. FOREST FLORIST 6. ARDENS GARDENS 7. COQUETTES ROSETTES

1. Movie dinner (1)

2. Cordage fiber plant part (1)

3. Georgia breakfast food (2)

4. Make reclining chair higher (1)

5. Nun's unadorned headcloth (2)

6. Actress Davis' landing piers (2)

7. Give German soldier soap and water (2)

ANSWERS:
1. REEL MEAL 2. JUTE ROOT 3. MACON BACON 4. RAISE CHAISE
5. SIMPLE WIMPLE 6. BETTES JETTIES 7. FRESHEN HESSIAN

1. Visitor search (1)

2. One who praises actress June (2)

3. Eel raid (2)

4. Discerning Alaskan native (2)

5. Indian nurse's animals (2)

6. Hermit's goofs (2)

7. Andrews Sister's cowpox viruses (2)

ANSWERS:
1. GUEST QUEST 2. HAVER RAVER 3. MORAY FORAY 4. ASTUTE ALEUT
5. AMAHS LLAMAS 6. LONERS BONERS 7. MAXINES VACCINES

1. Foot pain (1)

2. Be confident, Mr. Whitney (2)

3. Therefore concave fenders (1)

4. Ammunition for navy men? (2)

5. Wake up Juliet (1)

6. Due date for article title (2)

7. Funicello's tape cartridges (2)

ANSWERS:
1. TOE WOE 2. RELY ELI 3. HENCE DENTS 4. SEABEES BBS
5. ROUSE PROWSE 6. HEADLINE DEADLINE 7. ANNETTES CASSETTES

1. Without pots (1)

2. Saline milkshake (1)

3. Bad luck golf course (1)

4. Seer admirer (2)

5. Classroom-missile trap (2)

6. Eli's gaieties (2)

7. Showed remorse when crazed (3)

ANSWERS:
1. SANS PANS 2. SALT MALT 3. JINX LINKS 4. GAZER PRAISER
5. SPITBALL PITFALL 6. WALLACHS FROLICS 7. REPENTED DEMENTED

1. Mother's resorts (1)

2. Quite a mother (in London) (1)

3. Swift's mother and mother-in-law (1)

4. Mother's sacred songs (1)

5. Shrewd grandmother (2)

6. Russians' mothers (2)

7. Nurtures two famous brothers (2)

ANSWERS:
1. MAS SPAS 2. SOME MUM 3. TOMS MOMS 4. MOMS PSALMS
5. CANNY GRANNY 6. COMMIES MOMMIES 7. MOTHERS SMOTHERS

1. Keep dandy from falling down (1)

2. Go to party uninvited (1)

3. New kind of hut (2)

4. The best of the small and dainty (2)

5. Walk seen in fashion show (2)

6. Noise from carpenters (2)

7. Cicely's buffaloes (2)

ANSWERS:
1. PROP FOP 2. CRASH BASH 3. NOVEL HOVEL 4. PETITE ELITE 5. MODEL WADDLE 6. HAMMER CLAMOR 7. TYSONS BISONS

1. Steal a hit from Ty (1)

2. Strike out K.C.'s George! (1)

3. 1979 A.L. batting champ's victories (1)

4. Illegal pitches from one of "Gashouse Gang"? (1)

5. Our gratitude, slugger Ernie (1)

6. What batters had when Carl pitched (2)

7. Joltin' Joe's dance? (4)

ANSWERS:
1. ROB COBB 2. GET BRETT 3. LYNNS WINS 4. DEANS BEANS 5. THANKS BANKS 6. HUBBELL TROUBLE 7. DIMAGGIO ADAGIO

1. Keep out certain group of Scots (1)

2. Be rude to Peggy (1)

3. Army base mischief-maker (1)

4. Toe dance performed in French port (2)

5. Simon's cheek dents (2)

6. Silver Noncom (2)

7. Joyfully performed dramatic reading (3)

ANSWERS:
1. BAN CLAN 2. SASS CASS 3. CAMP SCAMP 4. CALAIS BALLET
5. SIMPLES DIMPLES 6. ARGENT SERGEANT 7. RECITED DELIGHTED

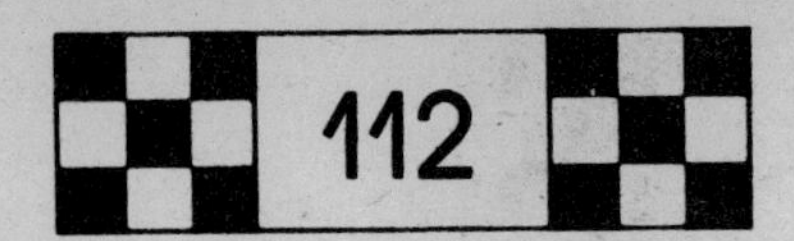

1. **Bando's buddies (1)**

2. **Tarts puff up (1)**

3. **Lorna's hunks of hair (1)**

4. **Research paper on experimental monkey (2)**

5. **Slightly angelic (2)**

6. **Records witty remarks (2)**

7. **Get stay of execution (2)**

ANSWERS:
1. SALS PALS 2. PIES RISE 3. LUFTS TUFTS 4. RHESUS THESIS
5. FAINTLY SAINTLY 6. TALLIES SALLIES 7. RECEIVE REPRIEVE

1. Bohemian gala (2)

2. 31 ounces (1)

3. Ms. Lauder in bad mood? (2)

4. Anatole of Paris' glib & rapid speech (2)

5. Secure oft-time office runner Harold (2)

6. Comfort Alabama governor (2)

7. Necessary means of identification (3)

ANSWERS:
1. ARTY PARTY 2. SHORT QUART 3. TESTY ESTEE 4. HATTER PATTER
5. FASTEN STASSEN 6. SOLACE WALLACE 7. ESSENTIAL CREDENTIAL

1. The adult Ms. Rivers (1)

2. Tease hair on animal's neck (1)

3. Irritable baby kangaroo (1)

4. Classifies common mineral (1)

5. Siberian drivin' dog sled (2)

6. What Twain's Prince does with Pauper (2)

7. Cocktail shaking? (3)

ANSWERS:
1. JOAN GROWN 2. FLUFF RUFF 3. POUCH GROUCH 4. SORTS QUARTZ 5. RUSSIAN MUSHIN 6. SWITCHES RICHES 7. LIBATION VIBRATION

1. Stag line (1)

2. Receive intimidating message (1)

3. Make yourself gorgeous, monkey (1)

4. Mealtime prayer on Apollo (1)

5. Char veranda (1)

6. Search light (1)

7. Steps between tee and green? (2)

ANSWERS:
1. BEAU ROW 2. GET THREAT 3. PRIMP CHIMP 4. SPACE GRACE
5. SCORCH PORCH 6. PROBE STROBE 7. FAIRWAY STAIRWAY

1. Wobbly dessert collapsed (1)

2. Geometrical rip (1)

3. Instrument for thawing (2)

4. Lowest form of bigot (2)

5. Groomsman groomer (2)

6. Seventh Day Adventist supervisor (2)

7. Suggestion for getting rid of garbage (3)

ANSWERS:
1. GEL FELL 2. SQUARE TEAR 3. DEICE DEVICE 4. BASEST RACIST
5. USHER BRUSHER 6. MORMON FOREMAN 7. DISPOSAL PROPOSAL

1. **Referred to aroma (1)**

2. **Pursues top pilots (2)**

3. **Stingy one's eye shades (2)**

4. **Gets rid of black and blue marks (2)**

5. **Ms. Burnett's kegs (2)**

6. **While awaiting forwarding (2)**

7. **Juliet's family's protective charms (3)**

ANSWERS:
1. MEANT SCENT 2. CHASES ACES 3. MISERS VISORS 4. LOSES BRUISES
5. CAROLS BARRELS 6. PENDING SENDING 7. CAPULETS AMULETS

1. Row harder! (1)

2. Aides' moment of hilarity (1)

3. Fashionable pig (1)

4. Pitcher bought more recently (2)

5. Name Justice Byron (1)

6. Exceedingly air-headed (2)

7. General Jackson's ring-ups (2)

ANSWERS:
1. MORE OAR 2. STAFF LAUGH 3. HAUTE SHOAT 4. NEWER EWER
5. CITE WHITE 6. MIGHTY FLIGHTY 7. STONEWALLS PHONECALLS

1. Tired little devil (1)

2. Age of lighted advertising signs (2)

3. Kamikaze pilot (2)

4. Almost-contemptuous expression (1)

5. Burned inside of mouth (1)

6. Cicely's teas (2)

7. A stitch in time to come (2)

ANSWERS:
1. LIMP IMP 2. NEON EON 3. ZERO HERO 4. NEAR SNEER
5. STUNG TONGUE 6. TYSONS HYSONS 7. FUTURE SUTURE

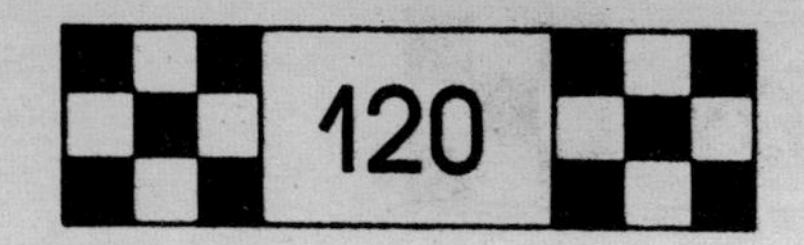

1. J-a-i-l-s (1)

2. S-h-o-u-t-s (1)

3. C-h-i-m-e-s (1)

4. V-a-l-l-e-y-s (1)

5. T-a-t-t-l-e-s (1)

6. A-r-t-e-s-i-a-n-s (1)

7. Intellectual overexertion (1)

ANSWERS:
1. SPELLS CELLS 2. SPELLS YELLS 3. SPELLS BELLS 4. SPELLS DELLS
5. SPELLS TELLS 6. SPELLS WELLS 7. BRAIN STRAIN

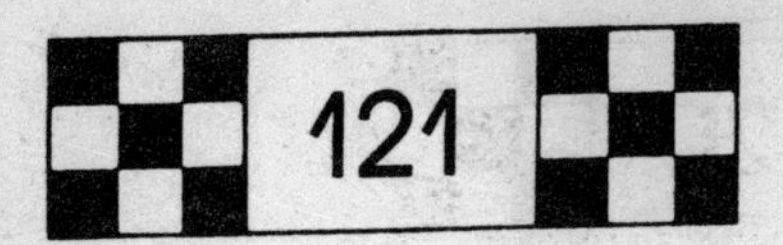

1. Heated crowd (1)

2. N.Y. Ranger's brief kisses (1)

3. Detroit Redwing's rakes (2)

4. N.Y. Islander's legends (2)

5. Phila. Flyer's golf clubs (2)

6. Montreal Canadien's cheese dishes (2)

7. Quebec Nordique's skeleton keys (2)

ANSWERS:
1. WARM SWARM 2. BECKS PECKS 3. DUGUAYS ROUES 4. SMITHS MYTHS 5. SUTTERS PUTTERS 6. MONDOUS FONDUES 7. STASKYS PASSKEYS

1. What a buddy! (1)

2. Pleads for bottom of barrel (1)

3. Famous rock group's sounds (1)

4. Disorderly tenant (2)

5. 60-second piano (2)

6. Come here, snake (2)

7. Diva Eileen's library nooks (2)

ANSWERS:
1. SOME CHUM 2. BEGS DREGS 3. STONES TONES 4. MESSY LESSEE
5. MINUTE SPINET 6. SLITHER HITHER 7. FARRELLS CARRELS